The Voice Of

My Soul

Published By

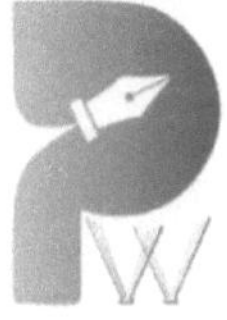

The Voice Of My Soul

Penned By

Hemlata Ruparam Mali

ABOUT THE AUTHOR

The Author, Hemlata Ruparam Mali, daughter of Mrs. Sundar Mali and Mr. Ruparam Mali. A Chartered Accountant aspirant by profession and Author by passion. She resides in Mumbai with her family. Hemlata is someone who just wants to bring smile on her readers' face through writings. She believes feelings can be better felt when penned. Also believes "Hurdles will always be there in life, all we need is to stay positive and achieve our goals".

Hemlata Ruparam Mali is the author of "The Hidden Treasure of Authors" anthology book. Also, a co-author in many anthologies.

You can follow Hemlata on

Instagram @disappearing_her

Email address: hemumali13@gmail.com

<u>ABOUT THE BOOK</u>

The Voice of My Soul is a handpicked collection of original pieces of poems written by Hemlata Ruparam Mali.

INDEX

<u>YOU</u>

Yes, you the person reading this!

It's totally fine to cry,

As crying makes you feel relieved,

Holding on too many emotions,

Eventually leads to tears.

It's totally fine not to be happy,

Life is full of ups and downs,

And the downs should be conquered courageously.

It's totally fine if you fought with your loved one,

Fights bring clarity,

And the heart speaks the truth.

It's totally fine if you don't feel like talking to
anybody,

There are days in life when you need your space.

So, you need to understand this,

It's totally fine to live life your way,

Now cheer up,

And feel the happiness of your birth.

<u>FEATHER - A LIGHT OF HOPE</u>

Coming to the end of the road,

A ray of hope was found through a feather,

Wishing again to reach the clouds,

As feeling the light weight of the feather,

Her soul took a step again to try loud,

And flew as high as the feather,

Touching the heights of success among the crowd,

Became a person with patience better,

All did the little feather changed her life and made
her feel proud.

<u>THE LONG JOURNEY OF LIFE</u>

Long is the journey,

Striving to achieve all the goals early,

Facing all the obstacles in between,

Never letting the negative vibes quit her dream,

Staying positive all the way,

Learning lessons in life.

Long is the journey,

Being a rollercoaster ride,

With ups and downs complied,

Listening all the taunts,

From uncles and aunts,

But having the family back,

As always her support system,

All she is trying is to achieve her goals.

Long is the journey,

Full of experiences is her life,

Surviving all the miles,

Here, she stands

Bold and brave going hand in hand,

Being a never stopping one,

Until she achieves her aim.

<u>HER PASSION</u>

Is it necessary to have someone as inspiration for

writing?

Someone whose writings are exciting

For her write-ups to be amazing, No it is

~ Her Passion ~

which made her write more and more,

And she became her own inspiration to the core,

As her thoughts in to words were poured.

<u>STRUGGLE - A PART OF LIFE</u>

Struggle

a part

of successful career

throughout the whole globe.

Life.

<u>FEARFUL STRUGGLES</u>

The world knew her as the most "fearless" person,

Unaware of the fears carried every day in her heart,

The fear of not making her parents proud,

The fear of not achieving her aim,

The fear of not having her name,

Yet, she chose to be a positive one as vowed,

And faced her fears becoming the bold one.

The world knew her as the most "fearless" person,

As her smile hid all her fears,

The fear of her tears to be seen,

The fear of her tongue speaking all the bitter truth,

Overcoming her fear she spoke the sooth,

And let her tears always be unseen,

Still got caught in front of her closed peers,

But they never reveal the things out to anyone.

<u>MEMORIES</u>

Years have passed,

Living those happy moments,

But it feels like yesterday was "The Day",

When she had cleared her entrance exam,

Her heart longs to relive those moments,

To see those tears of joy on her parent's face,

And that day has become an unforgettable memory
of happiness,

As some memories couldn't be captured,

But just felt and lived,

Same was her "The Day" memory,

Not captured but just lived to the fullest,

Each and every day that memory flashes in front of
her eyes,

And heart craves to relive them by clearing second
exam.

THE BITTER TRUTH OF LIFE

In the journey of life,

There lies a strange fact,

Where some forget to appreciate her act,

Though she has helped them in making their dreams come alive.

In the journey of life,

There are many struggles behind the scene,

But the achievements can only be seen,

As she hides the failures wearing a smile.

In the journey of life,

There are many ups and downs,

All we need to do is survive to be renowned,

And the important things should be prioritized.

<u>HAPPINESS</u>

Happiness is making my parents proud,

Feeling them reach the ninth cloud.

Happiness is seeing their tears of joy,

And making my parents enjoy.

Happiness is having their support always,

Be it a good or bad phase.

<u>FRIENDSHIP - A SPECIAL BOND</u>

Friendship is sailing in the same boat,

Yet, giving advices to each other to float.

Friendship is hiding one another's secrets,

And feeling the depth.

Friendship is just being a call away,

But not letting the hearts be away.

Friendship is teasing each other by their crush's
name,

And playing code words game.

<u>NATURE</u>

Nature, the most beautiful treasure,

Starting from the morning sunrise,

Lighting the whole world paradise,

And giving all enormous pleasure.

Nature being the most beautiful gem,

From the chirping of birds,

To the rain drops heard,

Growing into trees from the small stems.

Nature, the most beautiful treasure,

Full of waterfalls and mountains,

And being called the captain,

The reliever of all pressure.

<u>THE RAINY DAYS</u>

My heart sings,

Hearing the sound of rain,

Smelling the fragrance of sand,

Feeling the cold breeze,

Hugging me tight,

And making my face smile bright,

Seeing the greenery through trees,

Enjoying the weather holding one another's hand,

Also wishing for rain to come again and again,

Adding on to the memories my heart sings.

<u>THE SOUND OF WAVES</u>

Sound of waves gave her peace,

Brought the boisterous environment to cease,

Letting all her stress release,

And her happiness increase.

Sound of waves gave her peace,

Bringing smile on her face,

Lowering the race,

Being fierce,

Years by years.

Sound of waves gave her peace,

Setting her heart at ease,

Feeling the breeze,

And the moments freeze.

Sound of the waves gave her peace,

Being no other sound like these,

None other view as beautiful as sea,

Letting her feel free,

And be an adoree.

<u>THE MAGIC OF MUSIC</u>

Listening to music,

She entered her dreamworld,

Which made her feel optimistic,

As far from the hustle world.

Listening to music,

Gave her immense peace,

And she wrote an acrostic,

Which brought a smile on everyone's face.

Listening to music,

She understood the deep meaning,

And distanced herself from the toxics,

Finally started with the new beginnings.

<u>ADVENTURES</u>

Adventures were her escape,

All having a tape,

Risky ones were her favourite,

As exploring the bright,

However getting in to problems,

But never cribbing about the ones,

And strongly facing all,

Though being her parent's doll,

Ever-ready to ramble all around,

Experiencing her life's lost and found.

<u>BIRTHDAYS</u>

The day when she was born,

Is celebrated with joy,

Though being a girl rather than a boy,

And also the firstborn.

The day full of excitement,

For all family, friends and her,

Getting the best treatment,

As being the birthday of her.

From the day of being one,

To the day she turned twenty one,

The little baby enjoyed all her birthdays,

And looked beautiful on the special day.

<u>FOOD – EVERYONE'S FAVOURITE</u>

Love is food,

No one could say it a "No"

Whether be in a sad or happy mood,

All ate food slow slow.

Love is food,

Whether it's pizza,

Or roti from the homemade dough,

The real taste was having food tazza tazza.

Love is food,

From the mouth watering desserts,

To the plate licking delicious food,

Garnished with chocolate dark dark.

<u>THE EVERYDAY BLAMES</u>

They blamed girls,

For the incidents happening with them,

As short clothes showed their curves,

And expressed their condemn.

They blamed girls,

For roaming out late night,

As being a precious pearl,

To be stored and preserved in tight.

They blamed girls,

For back answering against wrong,

As 'yes' was the only word to be spoken by girls,

And bear the tantrum lifelong.

<u>WOMEN</u>

The human who worked day and night,

Not bothering about her life,

Being the house light,

Played all roles of working housewife.

The human who worked day and night,

Without getting any appreciation,

Doing all the things right,

Maintained all the relations with affection.

The human who worked day and night,

Though never got paid for her household chores,

Yet did all with her smile bright,

And adorned the house walls.

The human who worked day and night,

Leaving her dreams aside,

Still became everyone's reason of delight

And the best guide.

<u>BLACK IS BEAUTIFUL</u>

They complimented me as "Black girl (Kaali)"

Deprived of all beautiful features,

Liked by none,

Named the opposite of a pearl,

Known as the evil creatures,

Not good choice of anyone's son.

They were just hurting her deeply,

Unaware of how she felt by those evil compliments,

But she was a brave one,

Who fought against all alone only,

Finally proved that "Black is beautiful" and blessed,

Either a skin or a colour.

<u>INNER BEAUTY</u>

Was it necessary to be fair?

To have thick black hair

For everyone to like her, No it is

~ Her inner beauty ~

That mattered the most

But which couldn't be disclosed

As her colour

was first opposed.

<u>DOG – HER FOREVER COMPANION</u>

He was a tiny little baby,

With eyes open barely,

Over loaded with cuteness,

Far away from rudeness,

His face melted her heart,

Being a creature of astonishing art,

Slowly turning around in the cradle,

Looking like an angel,

Nature being playful,

Learning to walk gracefully

Her heart overwhelmed,

Looking at him drenched,

Big was he turning from the little baby,

Giving her the feel of being a mother,

Titled as a "Dogmother",

Gathering all the emotions together,

Only for her forever baby,

As the four-legged creature was her life.

<u>YOUR ABSENCE</u>

It's your absence,

Which made me realise my existence,

Right was my resistance,

Against your wrong insistence,

And, I finally learned to outdistance.

<u>LOVE - A PAINFUL LESSON</u>

Love

hurts you

once in lifetime

to make you strong.

Truth.

<u>SLEEPLESS NIGHTS</u>

Sleepless were his nights,

With plenty of thoughts in mind,

Staring at the moon's light,

Wondering about her kind.

Sleepless were his nights,

Remembering those moments,

Of planning the future bright,

And now, thinking whether it was real or fake
agreement.

Sleepless were his nights,

Missing her every day,

Though pretending to be alright,

Yet not believing it to be a play.

<u>LOVE PASSED BY</u>

For a long time has passed being separated,

Yet, feels like yesterday were the moments created,

Swiping those photographs,

Remembering your laughs,

Eyes holding on tears,

As not forgetting all the bears,

Yes, she missed him

But never wanted him back,

Despite being still in love.

<u>KARMA</u>

The reward of our seeds,

To be paid off once in life time,

For all the bad deeds,

No-one is forgiven for any crime.

The vicious circle,

Where the bad done comes back,

May have done by force or will,

And leaves a person with a crack.

The rewards of our seeds,

Sowing bad will reap bad ones,

And sowing good will reap good seeds,

Gets hold of everyone who ever runs.

<u>THE YEAR "2020"</u>

The cursed year,

Starting with Corona all over the world,

Leaving people in fear,

And many things observed.

The cursed year,

Further with earthquake in Delhi,

All feeling helpless standing alone here,

Only can pray for recovery slowly slowly.

The cursed year,

Outbroke into cyclone in Odisha and West Bengal,

And people were all in tears,

Feels as many things yet to be detrimental.

<u>SMILE</u>

Smile is the best thing,

When happy lightens your face,

And when sad hides your tears,

Shows someone's care,

And smiles with grace,

Said to be more beautiful than any diamond ring.

Smile is the best thing,

That can win many hearts,

Also make anyone's day as bright as sun rays,

In any bad phase,

And make new starts,

With a smile - the precious thing.

45